the Book
of
HER

Poetry Blog: www.amazulugaming.com
Instagram: Onepoeticgamer
Twitch: www.twitch.tv/onepoeticgamer

ISBN 978-0-578-91145-8

Published by
AmaZulu Gaming, LLC

Cover Art and Photographs by
Billy Williams, Jr.

Art work done by
Christopher James Rowland

Final Edition
Printed in the United States of America

Table of Contents

the prElude

11 minutes in, 11 hours later

HER (His Emotions Released)

Dedication

The gift of this book is that my soul knows all of
these poems are easily applied in reverse.
Remember always, your love is the same energy
you send to the person you choose to love.

This book is written for the soul of HER.

the prElude

for HER
(Poem #2)

I can recognize the beauty
from your energy
feel the way you sound
across piano keys and guitar strings
I create my own dream
where we make love on notes
played and written
scripted so that music does the talking
call that poetry speak
marathon sessions in which duets
flex the muse
please don't mind how
I'm in love with your sound
your rhythm equates my jazz notation
mixed components blend
science and nature creating magic
something never heard before
but feels so familiar
footprints made, found and followed
back to original state
a place our spirit came from
electro waves on sonic rotations
this is deity spontaneity
something kind of beautiful
like mistakes corrected by taking the next step
making the soul smile
passed on from one lifetime to the next
let's see the differences and enjoy the view
learning what love is continually

just by being you and me
see this sun shine
just…like…this.

for HER
(Poem #3)

Sweet like kissing you
to rhythm and blues
Marvin Gaye type crooning
moving my fingers onto your hands
embracing gently
simply, this is the butterfly feeling
at preteen age when
first discovering love,
less of self so we don't need make up
let's make up a fantasy
that turns true
tender roni, all up on me
if there are limits I'm feeling few,
not any that could stop this flow
this forward movement
attuned with power of another caliber
not normally manifested
less with guesses and more so complex
that it's only meant for us to get
breathe slow and take hold of
these intangibles provided,
nothing better cause there aren't any handles
lost control by choice since I need your free will
pen love in letters poetically
so words speak truth and comfort at the same time
flip the search so you come looking for me
even though we found us in each other
lover, I am at my peak

this feat is nothing less than extraordinary
carrying these thoughts when remembering
when remembering
when remembering.

for HER
(Poem #4)

Feel that trickle down your back
tears from blue skies fall like that
heaven bliss fused impact
boom so powerful I hope you stay intact
inside out, half empty
plenty of which you lack
tap wood three times, no superstition
this is based on facts
tic tac what's that
hiding behind those shades
laid eyes on you and the feelings amaz-
ing kick back, legs stretched
listening to heart string
voice sang its way to my soul
quite bold, truth be told
and this poem is the offspring.

for HER
(Poem #5)

This is my head
in your lap
listening to
smooth strokes
from your hand
across my face
for what seems like hours and
it feels like beautiful
warmth intended
as I could literally live
in the moment
on repeat, so soothing
to be pieced together
by spiritual stamina
in the physical
rubbing deep into
leftover tension
our energy answering
not to be found wanting
but I'm needing more
so much more
from you.

for HER
(Poem #6)

Your body curled onto mine
head under my chin
your scent fresh with
vanilla mint
as I wonder if
it's possible to taste your essentials,
essentially soul stimulus
pumping HER stimulant into my heart
and this is that Sunday morning feeling
in each other's arms
as I slow trace affection into your skin
with, air from your nostrils
bringing warmth to my chest
light reduced from shaded curtains
enough to enjoy highlights of you
softly my thoughts ease through
thankful we're side by side
with intentions to be here
for most of the day
or maybe, move wherever you go
not attached but fused
in between our perfection and flaws
so lovely are we.

for HER
(Poem #7)

Silhouettes of sounds and alchemy
created by way of voice
humming to the strings of my subconscious
playing from mind speakers
and, I'm happy to be here
in presence with dreams that reflect actual
noticing beyond senses
put it on everything
that I just felt a dragonfly's wings beat
meeting at the place where
tears are made from joy,
if you are looking for love
it's here
right there between
verses we believe unconsciously
without limitation
destiny meeting fate
then designing balance
somewhere within
me and you.

for HER
(Poem #8)

Make love songs for me
ones I'd keep on repeat
that I know speak
to the connection that people question,
played while I bathe
as you join in
let's take hold
of the rhythm that won't stop
this is no longer a phase
stay here for a moment longer
in this bass line
laced without explanation
despite how she sings
I mean, this is "dem tings"
slang that brings
words to speechlessness
if you could
show me, show me, show me
you know me so we
stay fixed on proposed ballads
that feel necessary
as she makes love songs
for me.

for HER
(Poem #9)

She strings melodies while I'm sleep
lullabies played live when I awake
she's cross legged in front of my face
love laced chords and keys
that sway through my mind
through my being
believing this to be the reason
the Earth spins on its axis
opposite of summer madness
glad this was waited for
smiles as she pours
tat-tat-tat-n-tat-tat-n-tat
tat-tat-tat-n-tat-tat-n-tat
so much in that my human existence
has shot to higher planes
where our flames sit looking at
our Earthly experience
something serious, seriously
let's not skip play
be it four or just the two of us
rock your love my way
and I hope you are ok with
how we currently are
even though we are the only ones looking
we're being watched by
a million stars.

for HER
(Poem #10)

I find that which is you aesthetic
something I hope to embrace
in every lifetime,
a dream love
with us as instruments
that can sing its song
somewhere within the passion
bearing fruits
as sweet as the word itself
and, in the beat of the moment
some call the rhythm of the night
dancing on lights in darkness
I find that which is you
beautiful.

for HER
(Poem #11)

Lights turned down low
close my eyes so
I feel the moment that much more,
I've imagined you here
like this, so many times
that I recognize the energy
literally, only needing you
to step through this picture
reminisce on the love we had in my dreams
then bring it to fruition
needing to give this to you
how ever it is you desire
taking you there because
you asked me to,
count this math while I place
you comfortably in position
for a memory,
living in the moment but choosing to remember
affection you gave the last few minutes
even after we're finished
I'll relive it
as we bask in this cuddle
happy to no longer having to hold
all of it in.

for HER
(Poem #14)

This isn't typical
so far from typical
what I'm feeling for you,
mind questions
can't be no second guessing
want to say it's love
but unreasoning passion seems
more like what it's passing for
still, don't follow the collective
not supposed to be what's expected
not sure what to call this
but I keep sprawling these poems
out the same side of my soul
right half of my brain
and you might not even compensate
the attention I allocate
and concentrate on giving you
that in which I'm showing you
and if it's meant
you'll notice, too.

11 minutes in
11 hours later

for HER
(Poem #16)

Here manifesting
this love, not the dreams of
self-served magic
I'd rather, share this polarity
between no place and everywhere
with you, then to
encounter well wished scenarios
that are short term studied
I got these, bottled elixirs
titled "poems"
filled with words like verbs
nouns and adjectives
compressed with brain steam
and feelings, I'm sending
by way of vibes your tribe made
when tapping percussion instruments
intrigued, I sat by the way side
awaiting your solo
as if the song you'll play is just for me
and you, maybe even the universe too
but I'll make do with the aforementioned
listen, you take my breath away
so I'm on borrowed time
for you to blow kisses my direction
just for use of oxygen,
the words I could say
were used to write this poem
for impressions I know you'd have
because that's what I manifested

from the beginning of this lyric
just to distract you long enough
to kiss your spirit
while you were looking.

for HER
(Poem #17)

Let's eclipse
phase the two of us
so waves of energy can reach peaks
that we'd exchange
then gain perspective
mix our elements
so fluid leaks, rivers crest
then overflows enough
to quench a distant thirst
producing ecliptic perfection
from our lips entwined
watch nature birth love
get high just observing our auras
paradoxal cataclysm
poured out as rainfall
that distinguishes yang from ying
as this is that deep part of the ocean
on the other side of the abyss
-pause-
maybe I should just ask you
to kiss me.

for HER
(Poem #18)
-One Night Only-

In a low light intimate box
she strummed the bass poetically
opposite of me
from a smoked filled room,
I sit upon a barstool
situated at an angle
apperceptive of the accompanying musician,
as I soft speak lyrics
in analytic scripture
from the book of HER.

for HER
(Poem #19)
-December Rain-

She sent waves of drizzle
til noon was an after thought
as I watched from two windows
time easing by,
atop my mind were thoughts
played soft like smooth jazz
that I chose to sit back and relax in
as the mist came
slipping through window screens
reminding me of the cool effects of her presence
one I need not a jacket for
as this is more like the nature of things
how it should be
at least for me when considering HER
a soulful lover
made music to my ears through natural sounds,
I'm in love - on some other level
defined by intuition
where souls speak
and when focused meet
quite non discreetly
if it pleases,
and I'm pleased with this current status
our bond of sorts through the elements
hoping you can sense the same
during this December rain.

for HER
(Poem #20)

You just look
as if you taste like pleasure
give me the experiences of tranquility
to the point
that bliss could be mixed with negative
and you'll find me asking
for cups of your balance
universal Milky Way cream added
as your particles contain flavored star dust
and, my soul is happy
with my intuitive drink of choice.

for HER

(Poem #21)

Our pattern is made up of sacred geometry
reoccurring yet unique
I speak, you reach within
and communicate the same
pain can be a choice
so let's choose to be happy
find quality in the time we keep
meet within somewhere deep
for the sweetest thing we've ever known
atoned all differences since
we came here, let me show you how I've grown
lone wolf that no longer walks alone
reap what's been sown
gentle winds are blown
and I'm shown this is the pattern for
what's considered sacred geometry
if x equals an unknown factor
then that's you + me = we.

for HER
(Poem #22)

Stars align on the inside of me
as I am part of the universe
so when watching distant lights
flickering in skies
that's you and I talking
just within reach, limitless
infinite are the ways in which
both mindful and unconscious
you move through my mind
hoping you find comfort in these words
this pillow talk, this mantra
used to put me in the train of thought
that focuses on you
it's what I do
to make time pass and stand still
then enjoy the moment,
as this is what I will remember
when having to separate
even if it's just a space of time
from you.

for HER
(Poem #25)

I'm in this state of mind
listening to opportunity make way
without the use of feet
unlooping the track
in favor of cross country
where thoughts could roam free
and maybe run into you
wondering, would it be rude if
upon meeting I move this
back to the future
so you remember
it's mid-winter
and time reflects projections with
me in you
or
you on me,
that's outside the box we just left from
inside were comfort sleeps with commitment
and everything is right when
nothing is left to be given
driven to the point
that I chose not to be a passenger
although I'm riding with you
so let's stay where we belong
as one,
because that's how it's meant to be.

for HER
(Poem #31)

If you are as sweet as you appear
then come be my brown sugar
comforting me like warm tea
you bring spring type feelings
delivered in angelic lullabies
hum me to sleep while we embrace
flocks of your hair underneath my chin
scents of coconut oil engulf me
I lay in your waves of silent expression
divine in your fingertips that
caress my skin on one hand
interlocking with the other,
I'm this close to contentment
since this is heaven on Earth
now that we're here
like this, just us, so close
to fulfillment
transcending from love
into souls that remembered forever
together, across the age of time.

for HER
(Poem #32)

While in observation of your image
I could taste your lips
embellished in their moisture
soft with a bit of gloss
and I feel the need for slow
reciprocated smooches
as we lay close enough were
our hearts palpitate to each other's rhythm
this vibe is the epitome of sensual
mixed with surreal
but this feeling, this listening
to the sounds made from
delicate endearments
it pleases me,
and I could - do this
for an extended bit
finding the night in your embrace
worth the currency of a moment spent.

for HER
(Poem #33)

This is the "act as if"
beyond the wish
where the draw in
are feelings being applied like thoughts
which creates moods that
moves me to believe
anything perceived in my mind's eye.
I'm so into you
it makes me wonder
if this is even human nature,
can't help but to seek divinity
inner me, enter the vicinity
of reality that evolved from my dreams,
she is the feeling of love unconditioned
driving me to release
uncivilized passions only seen
on a soulful level,
as access is forbidden unless aligned
and this is my line to you
to the other side of no comeback
no matter the choice made
freely this verse is given
with lack of expectations
if anything,
hopes lay in want of ascension
the lesson learned as this was scripted
your approval would only be a kiss
albeit, a desired one in the grand scheme

but maybe…
maybe this is the spring shower
many avoid not knowing
this is your invite
to dance that beautiful dance.

HER
(His Emotions
Released)

for HER

(Poem #34)
-a love deluxe-

Ms Adu plays in the background
while I lay in comforts that involve
thoughts of you,
against guitar strings her voice sings
allurement to my attention
watch me dance in equilibrium
through spirt we entwine
signs in clocks repeating statistics
that's fitted into my mind
imagining mountains moving
from the seed situated a few inches
within my chest,
can feel it when I wear it
like a tattoo around my essence
let's bank on the fact that
you'll feel this
before you'd ever see it coming
a surge of affection that
stands before you
waiting to be embraced
then released from timeline capsule
as stars shine in distant skies
happily, winking at you.

for HER

(Poem #35)
-Love in Secret-

I picked up on high vibes
transcended learned routines
and asked higher guides
for routes, paths, directions
on this experience
especially since this is a bit unexpected
sitting in dark places
gathering pulsations formed from
the ripple effect when we met
let this eave of thought
ease back unconscious programing
watch me,
spam these verses until you realize
I didn't come to play
yet at the same time
I put poetic notes online
in hopes you'll find
meaning somewhere in-between
strange dreams seem
to make connections for a lesson
in which you and I put
time in to spark a re-birth
unlock secrets that open doors to impossible
all because we trusted and believed.

for HER
(Poem #36)
-Watching Love Make Us-

You're my favorite on repeat
a dream I did not have to chase
an idea I will not have to push
a force I was not required to use
a day I need not save
the mirror that reflects me
mates that equal a soul
watching, as love makes us.

for HER
(Poem #37)
-Letters to U-

Let's invent memories
that I play back in my mind
to nourish our souls,
find another reason to create
wake up in the morning
to make physical manifestations
from dreams we played in
so vivid, I spend currency collected
from energy I balanced my love account with
got me, into whatever you're thinking
from trust funds my ancestors deposited
tuned in intuitive spirit
discovering something already found
now part of, time stamped
then mailed this directly to
U.

for HER

(Poem #38)

-Cycle Then Move in Reverse-

Let's live out this dream
in the mind of the universe
you and I meeting
brings together multiverses
here to converse with the use of verse
for a vision we've been envisioning
I'm listening to telepathic transmissions
and feelings in my gut when
my senses get to tingling
butterflies flapping so I get wind
of vibes emitting from love you're sending
through soul decisions that move
a step beyond intentions
I should mention then
negatives balance the outside from within
perspective depends
on who's telling the story
so let's go back from where we began
two friends meeting, that's multiple verses
in the mind's eye of their universe
living our dream to no end.

for HER
(Poem #39)
-Let's Play the Numbers-

She speaks math to me
loving, repeatedly
222's be
sometimes quadruple spiritually
she's missing me
when apart are we
so timely she
alerts me to see
11:11 digitally
I think it's really
beautiful how she feels me
non-physically
consciously manifesting
1 behind another 1 plus 1
we're focusing
meditative state
relating, debating eternity
abundantly giving
at 8, times three
that's 24 hours daily
you'll find her occupying
my mental place
want to kiss her face
as she speaks
math to me.

for HER

(Poem #40)

-Soul Song-

This is a soul song
what's used to reflect a muse
she knows this too
sitting in this room
where rhythms written to form
are shape shifting like liquids
in harmonic resonance
ancient love unconditionally waited on
served in multidimensional platforms
currently on a lifespan
to innerstand concepts
that go farther than scientific theory
be this light and sound transmission
we converse on, never separated
even when day dreaming at 3 pm
be that sixth sense feeling
nine times over, watch calculating
stimulus in water-based molecules
amplified by passion
light bringer, magnetically
pushing and pulling between poles
causing events on the horizon
where he awaits
in reflections of outer space
when playing this
soul song.

for HER
(Poem #42)
-Pass This-

Let's give a kiss
like true lovers in which
we exchange love in breath
and pass each other this.

for HER
(Poem #43)
-Watching in the Rain-

Here I am
watching you
walking in the rain
and, it's beautiful
because I know
I am in love with
your energy
and the thought to
tell you so
feels a bit desperate
to the point that
I can't let it
misguide me
if that even makes sense
either way, I didn't
and here we are
engaging in harmony
seeing the truth
fall through lies
and I, am watching you
walking in the rain.

for HER
(Poem #44)
-A Few Things-

We exchanged soft forms of love
through exercising patience
when misunderstanding
doing for the other
just for the feels given when surprised
exchanged looks between eyes
and these are a few reasons why
I love you.

for HER

(Poem #45)

-He and Her Meet-

Our meeting is a reunion of sorts
something that the world
didn't even know it was waiting for
of course, more important is
two beings being human, learning things
despite the fact that in this era
you're a beloved princess
and I'm labeled different
when casting around these titles
yet, let's not focus on blood lines
as you'll find I'm the pulse to your beacon
drawn in on scriptures by digits
similar to hieroglyphics
picture it in texts
that places coincidence with purpose
convert this until it works
since it's a pleasure to serve
imagine what happens when embracing
creative thinking and impossible when we converse
search my thoughts since I'm out of my mind
experience tranquility when our bodies align
combine this, with a bit of some of that
and one could pinpoint where we're at
fact is, I dreamed this fiction as a fan
to see if reality and my mentality
could emphasize the phrase "same difference"
this isn't some random method
based off scientific experiences

I really went there to get here
in order to present future endeavors
from past experiences
reject me now and I'll
just find you next lifetime
seeking oneness from our separation
lessons learned, no longer subtracting
the aforementioned differences
with the addition of this sentence in sequence
our numbers combined give us the sum
deep within feelings, hide not when I seek
ready or not here I come
light years worth of miles and
my heart still runs
just so I can get close to you
and do this...

About The Author

Billy Williams, Jr. was born to write poetry. Poetically knows as B-Dot and OnePoeticGamer, the life as a poet all started because of a girl back in 7th grade. Seeing he had a gift with words, he began to use his energy to produce poetry that spoke to various genres.

Hailing from Raleigh, North Carolina, Billy is a poet, coach, gamer, creator and an educator. The Book of Her is Billy's fifth book of published poetry, with more poetry books to be released in the near future.

If you want to find out more information about Billy's upcoming books, you can contact him by way of e-mail at onepoeticgamer@amazulugaming.com or sending a message to him from the following website www.amazulugaming.com. If you wish to know more about his gaming/streaming life, check him at www.twitch.tv/onepoeticgamer.

Social Media Contacts

Poetry Blog: www.amazulugaming.com
Instagram: Onepoeticgamer
Twitch: www.twitch.tv/onepoeticgamer

AmaZulu Gaming, LLC

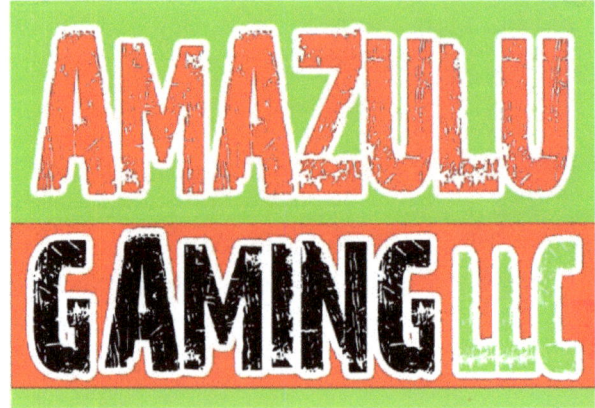

Poetry Books Written By One Poetic

Poetic Superhero

Everybody is looking for a hero. Poetic Superhero is here for you.

The I prElude I

In order to find we, HE must find himself before finding SHE.

His Emotions Released

This is written for Her…I'm glad I finally got Her attention.

School Dad

Poetry inspired by 16 years of working as an educator in elementary, middle and high school.

the Book of HER

33 poems for HER.

Poetic Flows - A Book of Rhymes (upcoming soon)

When I feel the flow, I let go with words.

Excommunicated (A Bard's Tale) (upcoming soon)

Exit wounds given by another can lead to one's salvation.

Leftover Love Poems (Future Release)

Sometimes you'll get things humanely wrong just so your soul can get right.

HER - The Collection (Poetry Anthology) (Future Release)

Includes works from The I pr.E.lude I, His Emotions Released and the Book of HER.

<u>Spoken Word By One Poetic</u>

Blue Room Mix Tape (upcoming soon)

www.ingramcontent.com/pod-product-compliance
Lightning Source LLC
Chambersburg PA
CBHW042145170626
46815CB00006BA/321